KAY THOMPSON'S ELOISE

Eloise and the Snowman

STORY BY **Lisa McClatchy**

ILLUSTRATED BY **Tammie Lyon**

Ready-to-Read
Aladdin
NEW YORK · LONDON · TORONTO · SYDNEY

ALADDIN PAPERBACKS
An imprint of Simon & Schuster Children's Publishing Division
1230 Avenue of the Americas, New York, NY 10020
The text of this book was set in Century Old Style.
Manufactured in the United States of America
First Aladdin Paperbacks edition October 2006
2 4 6 8 10 9 7 5 3 1
Library of Congress Cataloging-in-Publication Data
McClatchy, Lisa.
Eloise and the snowman / story by Lisa McClatchy ; illustrated by Tammie
Lyon.—1st Aladdin Paperbacks ed.
p. cm.—(Kay Thompson's Eloise) (Ready-to-read)
Summary: When snow starts falling in New York City, Eloise skips
breakfast to rush out to Central Park to build a snowman.
ISBN-13: 978-0-689-87451-2 (pbk)
ISBN-10: 0-689-87451-0 (pbk)
[1. Snowmen—Fiction. 2. Snow—Fiction. 3. Plaza Hotel (New York, N.Y.)—Fiction.
4. New York (N.Y.)—Fiction.] I. Lyon, Tammie, ill. II. Thompson, Kay, 1911–
III. Title. IV. Series. V. Series: Ready-to-read
PZ7.M47841375El 2006
[E]—dc22
2005030957

I am Eloise.
I am six.
I live at The Plaza Hotel
on the tippy-top floor.

This is my room.
If I am very, very careful,
I can peek out my window.

It is snowing!

"Nanny," I say,
"we must go outside."
"Not now, Eloise,"
Nanny says.
"It is time for breakfast."

"Breakfast can wait,"
I say.
Oh, I love, love,
love snow.

We cross the street
to Central Park.

I roll a ball of snow.
I roll another . . .
and another.

"Look, Nanny," I say.
"It is a snowman."

But something is missing.

I hail a driver
and his horse.
"To The Plaza at once,"
I say.

"Room service," I say,
"please bring me one carrot."

I race back to the snowman
and Nanny.

"Nanny," I say,
"do you like his nose?"
"Oh yes, dear," says Nanny.

But something is missing.

"Driver, away," I say.

Only the best tailors will do.
I get a hat, a coat,
a scarf, and gloves.

"Nanny, how does
my snowman look?" I say.

"Dashing, dear," says Nanny.
But something is missing.
"Back to The Plaza," I say.

"Eloise," says the manager. "How may I help you?"

"We must build my snowman
a house," I say.
"Send me
your best carpenters."

"Eloise, dear, his house
is lovely," Nanny says.

But something is missing.

My breakfast.
"Nanny, let's go home,"
I say.

Oh, I love, love, love snow.